ASTRAL PUNK

"In the fell clutch of circumstance
I have not winced nor cried aloud
Under the bludgeonings of chance
My head is bloody, but unbowed"
William Ernest Henley

ONE

Sam should've guessed things would end like this. That *she'd* end like this. Flames, green like emeralds, leapt up around her, each tiny burning tongue licking the walls in hunger.

Through the din of roaring heat and distant screams, she tried once more to break free from the tentacle wrapped tightly around her chest. She wheezed; a hissing. The wet, phlegmy crackle of her lungs filling with blood and saliva.

A fucking goner – that was what she was.

She squinted, vaguely making out Xavier's corpse through the smoke, where it lay on the floor. A second tentacle slithered towards him, the fleshy tendril's tip splitting open to reveal a solitary bony structure.

Sam gasped.

Sharp and pointed like a blade, the structure opened the man's gut with a quick, precise slash. Steaming innards splashed across the floor. Then, the tentacle slid inside.

Tunnelling, it spiralled upwards, coiling itself around his spine, emerging from his throat in a shredded explosion of flesh over shoulders.

"Xav—" Sam tried to whisper his name, but she was cut short. Her captor tightened its grip. Nearby, the bloated cadaver – the one she'd been studying only moments before – crackled. A macabre bonfire of spitting flesh. And beyond, the Esternati Chapter House blazed. As the underground edifice crumbled, the building's foundations buckled in places once thought sacred. A century of Esternati knowledge reduced to embers before her very eyes.

Men and women of the Order – Sam's fellow compatriots – were scattering. Running in panicked, disorganized circles, each shouting, screaming to one another through the smoke. A wooden beam snapped free overhead. Those caught beneath vanished in a black plume.

If there was a deeper pit inside her, Sam sank into it. She bit hard on her lower lip. In front of her, Richard, one of her closest friends in the Order, let out a strangled cry.

The fallen beam held him pinned. He bellowed, coughing up blood, his nails splintering against the wood as he fought desperately to get out from under its weight.

Richard was dead.

He just didn't know it yet. Beneath the beam, his body, split in two.

Blinking tears from her eyes, Sam swallowed, and the thing squeezed her tighter. Its suction cups throbbed, feeding off her despair. Sam's flailing protest pushed her to fading. The world became muffled, distant, echoing. Only the pain remained. It beckoned her, calling her to retreat someplace safe. Somewhere in her mind.

A mouldering, run-down apartment.

A static-flushed TV surrounded by mountains of VHS tapes.

Here, she could hit play on the re-runs of her life.

Here, she could watch until the final credits rolled.

Such a temptation might've worked on the uninitiated. Instead, Sam weaponized the pain, letting it anchor her, awakening her Far Body. Seconds ticked by. The autopsy room started to sway. The air itself was moving. Slow steady puffs at first, in and out, in and out. Then it sped up. Rapid. Hyperventilation. Panic. Faster. Faster. Fluttering invisible murmurings. The roaring heat. The screams of her comrades. The rumble of distant thunder. Each sound dulled. Beneath it all…

A second heartbeat.

Da-Dum, Da-Dum.

   Da-Dum, Da-Dum…

The snap.

The shift.

Sam hung midair. Weightless. Watching her own body as it dangled in the creature's twisting arm. A puppet without its puppeteer. The world's vibrant and furious tones fizzled out, overtaken by the muted shadows of the *Psychosphere.* Only the soft, mauve glow of her aura remained. Near the base of her stomach, it parted slightly, allowing a thin, silver umbilical cord to extend across the room, maintaining Sam's connection with her bloodied and battered meat-suit. This was her tether. The mythic cord anchoring her in this reality… and the next.

Through the haze, Compatriot Darlene stumbled into the autopsy room. She was soot-streaked and bloodied. The jagged scar on her face looking angrier than ever. An old battle wound, gifted to her by the claws of a festering ghoul, somewhere in the ancient ruins of Iram. It itched and stung in the presence of astral corruption, like a canary in some occulted coal mine. Strange then, that on tonight of all nights, the scar had remained calm until things were far too late.

Seeing Sam's empty body, Darlene frowned. She drew a gleaming knife from her belt, gripping the hilt till her knuckles drained of color. The blade itself was ornate and ritualistic; the hilt engraved with a bushel of tangled lavender. Charging, Darlene flung herself at the appendage, stabbing her dagger down upon the slick, rubbery flesh. It resisted at first, but then, with a little extra push, the blade slid through the outer membrane, burying itself deep.

The creature recoiled, letting Sam's shell drop.

Air rushed back into her lungs like a vortex. Her Far Body followed. Swimming through thick, invisible currents, she awoke alive, gasping and pawing for breath on the blood-soaked linoleum floor.

A fleeting victory. But a victory none-the-less.

Enraged, the tentacle whipped around. Seizing Darlene by the right leg, it hoisted her high. The woman roared in defiance before she was slammed hard against the floor.

Once.

Twice.

Three times.

Four.

A final, sickening crunch silenced her.

With a groan, Sam opened her eyes, clambering onto hands and knees. The wounded tentacle continued to thrash, sending stray surgical instruments clattering.

It's distracted.

But before Sam could take advantage of this, a violent crash elsewhere drew her attention. The body. The one only moments ago she'd been dissecting. It convulsed. Gyrated. Sat up on the mortuary slab.

Its shoulder muscles twitching, the body dropped feet to floor and stood. Bending backwards, its bloated abdomen curved unnaturally towards the ceiling. Its arms stretched out towards the floor. Shoulder sockets popped loudly as the corpse's bald head rolled, coming to hang upside down, along the top of the spine. Lifeless eyes became glassy, blank orbs. The corpse opened its mouth and shrieked. In response, the tentacles retracted, returning to their hiding spot inside the dead man.

Lumbering forward, upside down and on all fours, the cadaver closed in, pouncing like a predator. It was in that moment an explosion rippled through the building from somewhere above. Body parts. Chunks of broken concrete. Shards of glass. All flew wildly throughout the underground space. A sharp ringing filled Sam's ears. She was still alive. Still alive. Still alive… The blast had overturned the mortuary slab. Like a knight's shield, the smooth hunk of stone protected her. Grasping her side, Sam crawled through rubble, coughing and choking on mushrooming white dust.

What the fuck was that?

The reanimated corpse lay on its back, near the exit. It shuddered and shook. Black ichor leaking from its mouth, formed a dark pool on the ground.

Retrieving Darlene's blade, Sam gritted her teeth, dragging herself forward. She reached the body, letting out a huff of exertion. Crawling on top, Sam used what strength remained in her legs to pin the corpse long enough to take action. Raising the knife high, she plunged it downwards, embedding the silver tip into the revenant's pallid forehead.

The corpse shrieked. The black ichor, no longer confined to its mouth, poured from its eyes. Sam let the blade sit there while she focused her attention elsewhere. Drawing back slightly, she located the festering stomach wound from which the tentacles had first burst. With a roar, she shoved a fist inside.

Cold, slimy sausage shapes, each intestine parted for her fingers as she searched for an undulating mass hiding inside.

"Fuck you!" she shouted, her hand locking around a foreign, quivering shape. Ripped from the cavity, the Astral Parasite now looked surprisingly small. Gone were its huge, slippery tentacles. Instead, only a semi-spherical, starfish-shaped lump, shaking with terror, remained. Oh, how the tables had turned. A single eyeball darted, slit pupil blown wide.

This is it?

Sam held up the creature and stared.

How could something so small have caused all of this?

Then, she gagged.

The smell of the entity started to waft into her face. Unwelcome and obnoxious. Her nostrils flared. Rusted coins… mixed with charcoal? Coffee too black, too bitter, a top note of floral blue mould… Sam had smelt this many times, but it never got easier. Never became normal. None of this shit ever fucking did.

She snarled, letting the stench pass over her. It was time for some well-earned revenge.

Forcing her thumbs into the creature's cyclopean eye, Sam's nails slid in deep, passing through quivering jelly, then deeper still, until the entire socket burst. Translucent goo flooded her palms. She let the carcass fall.

Having borrowed its mass from a human anchor, this parasite had managed a powerful physical form. But now? Disconnected by force, it would quickly dissolve. Without an anchor, the trespasser's Far Body was vulnerable. The *Great Sigil*[1] would recognize it in an instant. With recognition came judgement. And with judgement…

Banishment.

Eviction.

"Alright! Let's make this quick!"

A man's voice, out of the blue, in the main office. Authoritative. Invigorated by a touch of madness. Gun metal shimmered briefly through the smoke. Sam pulled herself back, hiding from view.

"Got a live one over here!" a second man shouted.

---

1 *The Great Sigil: An unfathomably ancient and possibly autonomous structure believed to envelop our dimension. Visible only from the Astral Plane, its origin and function remain unknown — even to the Esternati. Across the centuries, the Esternati, Altiorem, and countless others have attempted to study it, with little success. Some claim it predates time itself. Many regard it as one of the last great mysteries of our realm.*

"No! Please!"

Cold sweat formed at the base of Sam's spine. That was Patrick. Eighteen years old. A transfer acolyte from the London Chapter House. A compatriot in training. The poor kid. She'd often spied him staying in the Chapter House late, re-reading 15th century manuscripts, preparing for exams.

BRAP! BRAP! BRAP!

A spray of bullets rippled through the boy. His plea for mercy ended in an instant.

Sam wanted to scream. To let loose a war cry. To charge at these motherfuckers. Make them pay. Patrick was a child. Now he'd never graduate. He'd never become a fully-fledged compatriot. He'd never fall in love. Never experience heart break. Never knowing the pure wonder of looking upon ancient and glorious lands. Sam resisted the cry burbling in her throat. She'd avenge him. But payback would have to wait.

Who the fuck are these guys?

Limping from the autopsy room, Sam snuck towards the intruders. Water spluttered down from above as the building's sprinklers finally kicked into action, dousing the remaining flames. It wasn't much, but enough to flood the room with steam. She could use this as cover. Get to safety. Plan her next move. She stole another glance.

There were four of them, moving through the building with semi-automatics in hand, scanning for survivors. It was hard to make the gunmen out in the gloom, but none looked familiar. Over the years, the Esternati Order had made its fair share of enemies. Sacrificial cults, obscure sects, and mystery religions.

These guys were different.

Most occultists were theatrical. Men and women obsessed with robes, hoods, and costume jewellery. None of that here.

They were all white, though Sam noted a strange blue tinge to their skin. A variety of magical symbols were tattooed in organized patterns across their shaved heads. Each man dressed in military-style uniforms. Camo pants, sweat-stained singlets, bullet-proof vests. Their muscular arms proudly displaying countless red and angry scars, spanning wrist to shoulder. If they *were* cultists, tradition was the last thing on their minds. No. More like militia. Neo-Nazis. Para-military.

These men had no interest in messing around. This wasn't random. Not the work of opportunists. Every security protocol the Order had, these guys breached. They hadn't stumbled into this. They'd planned it. Waited. For tonight. The parking garage corpse and its astral trespasser took care of the busy work. These fuckers simply stepped in for clean-up.

Sam shifted her weight, her boot nudging against rubble. The desk wobbled. A half-empty coffee mug precariously close to the edge toppled and fell. It bounced, clanged loudly against a metal desk-fan before coming to rest in the dirt.

Sam cursed.

One of the gunmen snapped his head around. Barking at the others, he raised his weapon.

"Got movement!"

Sam didn't wait. Pushing off from the ground, she bolted, ignoring the pain radiating through her chest.

"Get her!" someone yelled before firing.

Keeping her head down, Sam ran, her heart hammering in her ribcage as a hail of bullets tore past. Reaching the exit tunnel, she wrenched open the door and fled.

Several minutes later, Sam emerged within the Midnight Laundromat. Flames roared hot up here, turning metal washing machines red. Piles of soapy clothing spilled out, steaming. Weaving through the chaos, Sam took the back door into a side alley.

With a moment to herself, she leant her head against the brickwork. She needed a moment. Just a few seconds for the rain wash her skin clean.

The body…

The body, you fucking idiot!

Her shoulders sank; Sam pinched her skin. Tiny dots of red to rose to the surface.

You should've known!

You should've seen what was coming!

But she hadn't.

And as a result, her whole world got fucked.

Colleagues – friends and companions through the weird and profane – all dead. Not just dead. Eviscerated.

A sob, low and trembling escaped her lungs. Her hands moved on their own, slapping against the brick. Fingers stiffened, scraping broken and blood-caked nails down hard lines of mortar. As Sam fell into a squat, her arms stretched upwards, grasping, reaching for... what? Nothing. Anything. Something.

A release.

Her stomach convulsed. Dropping her arms, Sam turned and hurled against the rusted dumpster; the world tilted and she gagged again. Pain lanced through her abdomen, thought smeared thin. Somewhere inside, she became very small – an observer to the body's desperate work. The horror of it was pure and absolute, and in that absoluteness there was a strange, terrible calm.

Once the contents of her stomach stopped flowing, Sam pressed her back against the neighbouring building and crumpled. She closed her eyes. In the dark, Xavier screamed. Then, the wet crunching sound of Darlene, beaten over and over again into a silent pulp.

Eyelids flicking back open, Sam clenched her fists and slammed them against concrete.

She should've called an emergency evacuation the second she'd spotted something strange.

But no.

She'd been caught up in the mystery of it all. Too invested in a potential Altiorem conspiracy to think straight. All of that could've waited. Could've been explored at a different time. Whoever *was* responsible dropped that body on them as a distraction, and Sam – for all her pride at being the best and brightest Esternati in Ghostward – fell for it hook-line-and-sinker.

Tonguing a gash inside her cheek, she let the copper taste coat her throat. Xavier said Compatriota David left early. The head of their Chapter House, MIA. She'd need to find him. Get to a safe house and try to make contact. If he was still alive. He hadn't been there when shit hit the fan, so maybe there was a chance…

A way for the Esternati to rebuild…

Sirens howled a few blocks off. The city's emergency services kicking into action. Sam steadied herself, swallowing another lump in her throat. She stood and walked towards the main street.

Even at this hour, a small crowd was beginning to form on the road out front. The citizens of Ghostward looked on, mystified by the belching flames. Across the street, two more gunmen exited a parked van, rushing towards the laundromat's doors.

Doing her best to look casual, Samantha Lockart – last of the Esternati Order - limped quietly, quickly into the night…

TWO

Waldorf Tower, one week later.

Rain hit the concrete like teeth chattering. For a split second, the building lit up like a flare – jagged edges, elaborate effigies and grisly gargoyles illuminated in stark relief. Strange shapes, meant to inspire awe, seemed now to move and contort with an insidious nature before sinking back into the shadows.

In a narrow passage between two smaller buildings nearby, the dark-man watched. Tendrils of shadow obscured him. Each flickering, inky black whisp moved energetically around his form. They floated upwards like soda bubbles, each one stretching out then separating from their source. Evaporating in thin trails above his head. Within this shadowy camouflage, the dark-man's eyes were human. Small and rounder than most. Baby blue. Tiny flecks of amber around the iris. They were soft. Perhaps even kind.

But the dark-man was not.

He was not kind.

He knew this.

Even when he pretended otherwise.

Even when he believed his own lies.

Not that he often had the chance to be kind. The dark-man was a loner. He'd tried to make friends – he was still trying. But those rare exchanges never ended well. He'd offer his heart to somebody, and they'd tear it up. Act like he was nothing special. Like he was a loser – or worse – a monster! So, the dark-man would reveal to them his gift. He'd show them the suit of shadows and the magic paint. They'd meet his Mistress. Each new friend had to be introduced properly, just like she'd shown him. That was usually when they got scared. The dark-man didn't like that. Fear made them leave. And it was their going that hurt the most. But what was he to do? Abandon the Mistress? The dark-man couldn't even imagine how. The Mistress was a gift; she could make his wildest dreams come true.

Mother's milk, and all that shit...

The catch? He needed to realize her dreams first. At least, that was what the man had told him.

The dude with the pointed teeth and a tangled mullet. The one on the bike who wore a tattered blue denim jacket. He'd come to the dark-man at his lowest, like an angel descending from on high. The biker believed in the dark-man. What's more, he *saw* him for who he truly was. The biker understood the pain in the dark-man's heart, understood what he was capable of. The biker accepted him. Handed over the tools needed to bring silence to the endless weeping.

The biker visited twice more. The first time, almost a month ago, the dark-man cried when he saw him. He'd worried they'd never cross paths again. Before the words even left the biker's mouth, the dark-man let loose an emphatic YES!

The request?

It hadn't been pretty.

Moving some bloated, cut up dead guy from one location to the next.

The dark-man did as he was told.

He knew not to ask questions.

The second visit – two weeks back – had been much nicer, though the request equally bizarre. He'd asked the dark-man to observe a local community, a bunch of disenfranchised kids. These teens congregated at different venues across the city most weekends. They wore all black, had piercings and tattoos. Their music was a mess of distorted guitars and stomach-wrenching screams. They called themselves "hardcore", but the dark-man didn't really get why. To be honest, he didn't get much of anything they did. The kids seemed angry… or sad. The angsty tunes they clambered around spoke to him though. The lyrics – told through shouts – were almost indecipherable but resonated. They prompted a question, formless and abstract, deep within his withered soul.

"Keep an eye on them," the biker had said. "Watch for anything out of the ordinary."

"And what about friends?" the dark-man asked. "Can I make any friends?"

The biker's face shifted. His wolfish grin fell flat, lips tightening around pointed canines.

"No friends in *that* crowd," the biker replied, voice low. "Not yet."

The dark-man panicked.

"What about the Mistress? I still need her gifts. And she's always hungry…"

"Find your offerings *elsewhere*," the biker replied. "We don't eat where we shit, and you, my friend, are about to shit a lot."

The biker leaned in close. So close that the dark-man could feel his breath, warm and sour, like burning sugar.

"You said not yet."

The biker chuckled. "When She marks them, you'll feel it. But until then… look. Don't touch. We don't want to spook the nest."

Look, don't touch.

The punks were off-limits.

Not forever. Just… for now.

He could wait. He'd *try* to wait.

But as the dark-man would soon come to learn: those kids smelled sweet.

Irresistibly sweet.

Especially after a night of mosh pits, spin-kicks and flying fists …

From his hiding spot between the buildings, the dark-man blinked, slow and hungry like a great white. He'd been good. He'd been *so* good. Ever since he'd started watching, he'd obeyed the biker's rules. No touching. No talking. No new friends. Just him and the Mistress, drifting between shadow and light. He'd follow those little, black-clothed creatures as they moved from gig to gig. He'd follow them like a loyal hound.

But it was boring.

So boring.

God, was it boring!

Until tonight.

The boy and the girl weren't like the others. They seemed to be siblings. The girl he'd first clocked at the Discord only a week back. The boy… The dark-man wasn't sure where he'd come from, but he was alluring, too. The dark-man had kept tabs on them ever since the funeral. Now, here they were, stepping through the stormlight of Waldorf Tower like it meant something. He didn't know why they mattered, but they did.

The tower above was affluent, fancy even. A far cry from dingy venues and house parties. It was too tall, too clean, too sharp.

It reeked of purpose.

The dark-man's shadows curled around him, twitching with a life of their own. He wanted to touch these two, but he wouldn't. He *couldn't*. He needed to prove to the biker he was worthy. But they'd stirred the itch. The one behind his eyes. The one that would not stop unless he scratched. It had been with the dark-man his entire life. It was the voice that cried out for "friends," long before the Mistress arrived.

The dark-man wiped sweat from his brow and twiddled his hands in anxious anticipation. He couldn't play with these two, but perhaps he could play with someone else. Someone easier. Someone who had the band t-shirts and facial piercings but wouldn't be noticed or missed.

Yeah.

He could get away with it. He'd find someone to scratch the itch. He'd keep them a secret. From the biker *and* the Mistress.

What they didn't know wouldn't hurt them, right?

With a ripple of smoke and ink, the dark-man vanished, falling like liquid to the pavement, travelling through the night as he hunted for prey.

✦✦✦

The thunder above rolled low and wide as Jessie and Elijah darted across the carpark. Ahead of them, the tower loomed, upper windows flickering faintly through a curtain of rain. In silence, the twins approached. As they neared the courtyard, Jessie reached out, stopping her brother with a hand to his chest. Something. Up ahead. A shape, silhouetted by the light inside. Then, a narrow beam, swooping out towards them.

"Get down!" Tightening her grip on Elijah's shirt, Jessie yanked him behind a rust-spotted Honda. They crouched and shivered, the smell of wet asphalt burrowing into their nostrils. Across the way, a uniformed police officer stood beneath a soggy awning, glowing torch in one hand, cigarette in the other. He was young, weaselly looking, staring into the night with tired, beady eyes. A police-issue revolver hung from his waist in a black leather holster. The cop's posture was tense, but exhausted. A man who'd worked too many hours and received too few breaks. The illuminating beam slowed to rest over the siblings hiding spot. For a moment, the officer squinted in their direction. Searching but finding nothing of interest, he shrugged, tapping ash from his cigarette. Behind him, the lobby hummed with electrical warmth. Yellow police tape crisscrossed the revolving doors, fluttering in the breeze like torn ribbons. The shreds partially covered a large notice taped haphazardly over the entrance. It'd grown warped from the rain, but the header – written in big, red letters – was still legible:

BY ORDER OF THE GPD:
NO ENTRY WITHOUT PERMISSION.
INVESTIGATION IN PROGRESS.

The finer details of the notice were too far off. Those words bled together. Jessie snuck a look at her brother, noticing his tangled hair matting in clumps against his forehead. It'd looked the same all those years earlier. That night. The worst of their lives so far. He'd come inside when the soft flurry of snow turned into rain, washing away their afternoon snow angels. Jessie was in their kitchen, a young girl, heating up oven pizza when the doorbell rang…

Jessie shut the memory away. Elijah was focused; his eyes trained on the officer ahead with grim resolve. His white, tightly clenched knuckles peeking out from beneath his jacket sleeves.

"Oi!" Jessie whispered, holding up her hand and signalling him to stay low.

"D-dad's already buried," Elijah hissed back. "What are they still d-doing here?"

Another boom of thunder passed through them, growling and shuddering as it rolled across the parking lot.

"What about the fire escape?" Elijah asked. "Should take us right to Dad's floor."

Nodding, Jessie peered over the vehicle's hood. The officer was preoccupied, shaking and tapping his flashlight as it flickered unreliably against the tower walls.

"Now!"

The twins began to run, still crouched, past the entrance and towards the side of the building.

BOOM!

They rounded the corner, pressing themselves flat against the brickwork beneath the fire escape's rusted frame. The ladder's lowest rung was still hoisted above their heads, chained in place and slick with condensation. Reaching up, Elijah's fingertips brushed cold metal. He jumped, grunted, managing to snag the edge with both hands. But as soon as he started to pull, the ladder let out a high, splintering *CREAAAAK.*

Jessie flinched.

Her eyes darted back to the cop at the entrance. "Wait!"

Elijah froze, his arms straining. The ladder hung half-extended, groaning weakly like a dying cat. They listened. Another rumble building in the sky. Low and far away, it reminded Jessie of the Ghostward tube-line. Of carriages screaming as they charged along rattling tracks into claustrophobic voids.

"Time it with the thunder."

Elijah glanced skyward, his clothing soaked, the cold piercing his bones.

BOOM!

Another deafening crack from the heavens. With a growl, he yanked the ladder the rest of the way. Iron legs hitting concrete with a muffled *clang*.

Scrambling, the twins began their ascent. Elijah's lean frame pulled ahead. Jessie followed just below, her steel-capped boots sliding awkwardly.

"F-fourth floor, right?"

"Yeah. Big window."

By the time they'd reached the right landing, both were panting. Their rising body temperatures battling the pervasive chill in the air. Stepping onto the narrow balcony, Jessie joined her brother outside a large set of glass panels. Inside, a view into their father's home.

"It looks empty, but..." Cupping his hands around his eyes, Elijah continued, "...the w-window's locked."

"Out of the way."

"Wha-?" Elijah scrambled as his sister kicked through the glass, showering the carpet inside with thousands of sparkling shards.

"Jesus!"

Brushing the remaining jagged pieces from the frame, Jessie grinned.

"After you, little bro."

Their father's apartment had always been a mess, but never anything like this. A black and white patterned lounge-suite lay turned on its side, shoved violently against a wooden coffee table. Loose papers lay scattered across the living room, overflowing from an old storage cabinet leaning precariously against the doorway to the hall. Their father's chunky TV hissed incessantly with a snowstorm of static. It was the only sound in the apartment, aside from the occasional scratching and scampering of rats in walls.

"What the hell happened here?" Jessie asked, stepping cautiously through the room. Spotting something within the mess, Elijah leant over to retrieve an empty green bottle. Shaking the last dregs of whiskey from it, he held it up to the moonlight.

"Glenlivet. Guess D-Dad started d-drinking again."

"ABSOLUTELY, I HAVE A PROBLEM, LUCY! AND IT'S NOT ME SIPPING FROM THIS FUCKING GLASS! YOU WANNA KNOW WHAT MY PROBLEM IS? IT'S YOU! YOU AND THOSE GODDAMN KIDS OF OURS! I'M TRYING TO DO MY JOB, AND ALL I GET ARE THESE FUCKING COMPLAINTS! HOW BAD OF A HUSBAND I AM. HOW

BAD OF A FATHER I AM… IF IT WEREN'T FOR ME, YOU'D ALL BE…"

That shouting, now years old, pierced through a closet door. Furious and drunken, the words reached inside. Elijah just wanted a good spot. Somewhere his sister wouldn't think to check. The best hide-and-seek location in the house! When Jessie finally discovered him there, weeping into a collection of leather dress shoes, Dad had already left to go driving, and Mom? She'd locked herself in the bathroom, shower running, hot steam escaping into the hall. The memory hadn't happened here, but that didn't matter. Elijah carried it wherever he went.

Unfortunately, the present had no interest in their father's well-documented struggle with alcoholism. Ignoring the bottle, Jessie stepped past her brother and continued to explore.

"Come on. We need to check everywhere. There's gotta be something the pigs missed."

"Or hid."

Jessie looked to her right, down towards the apartment's entrance. The door had clearly been forced. Their father was a careful man, yet all the locks and chains hung broken and loose. Another flash filled the narrow passageway with momentary light: bullet holes along the walls. She turned, imagining the path the intruder must've travelled. Her eyes settled on the door, ajar to her left: their father's study. Off-limits and out-of-bounds to them as teenagers, it now called out – *come closer. Come see what I've hidden...*

"I always preferred the townhouse on Preacher's," Elijah muttered dejectedly, breaking his sister's concentration.

"Dad needed something smaller."

Elijah scoffed.

"He n-needed a p-p-place that didn't remind him of Mom."

Ignoring him, Jessie reached the study door and pushed it gently open. As her eyes adjusted, her face contorted. If the living room was a mess, then the study was a literal warzone. It too had been ransacked – by the police, or someone else. She couldn't tell which.

Tattered blinds hung from the windows to the left; half ripped from their hangers. Their father's bookshelves lay flat on the floor, his collection of old tomes sprawled and covered with dark spots.

Blood.

The oak desk at the back of the room was similarly stained. More papers, torn and screwed up, cascaded over it, the leather desk chair thrown into a corner. A large, brownish smear occupied the back wall like a center piece. Like modern art, proudly displayed and titled: *Portrait of a Splattered Brain.*

"Oh..." Elijah whispered as he joined his sister.

This was where their father died. Seated at his desk, entombed in research, his final thoughts sprayed across the ceiling. Jessie closed her eyes, squeezing them tight. She swallowed. Dad was a prick, but this… He didn't deserve this, no matter what he'd done.

"Try not to think about it too much." Words. Advice. To Elijah? To herself? Jessie kept focus on her brother as she said this, but her voice had gone soft, like she was trying to calm her own reflection.

"Remember, we have a job to do."

"Y-yeah…" Elijah turned away, swiping at his cheeks with the back of his hand.

Jessie scanned the room again. She didn't know exactly what she was looking for, but there had to be something. Anything that stood out, that didn't look right. A clue. It had to be hiding in plain sight. It had to be…

There.

On the right.

The corner of the room behind the desk, opposite Dad's chair. It was different. Strange. Disruptive. Unlike the plain-coloured wallpaper decorating the rest of the office, this section fucked with the flow.

"Odd…"

Jessie approached. A pattern. Decorated with small, geometric triangles, clustered together and coloured purple like tiny flowers.

"Is that a… l-lavender blossom?" Elijah asked. "Dad didn't have the b-best of taste, b-b-but—"

His words cut short. Jessie pressed her fingers lightly against the pattern, prompting a loud *click*. Moving gears clanged through the study. The twins stepped back. The wall swung open, revealing behind it a secret chamber.

The shadows inside were inky. Jet black and heavy. Not just the absence of light, but… the presence of something else. Something… *other*.

"Come on…"

Jessie stepped across the threshold. They stood together for a moment, allowing the darkness to soften. At first, it looked disappointingly barren. A lone wooden bench sitting in the middle – bare, except for a small mechanical model of the solar system. Several filing cabinets lined the chamber, each gathering dust.

The room contained nothing else.

Crossing the floorboards, Jessie approached one of the cabinets, pulling the top drawer open. Inside, a collection of yellow manilla folders, each containing paperclipped reports on subjects Jessie could only describe as… insane. Strange sketches of unsettling creatures. Bizarre occult symbols, a mixture of notes in English and Latin down the margins. There was some kind of code, strewn throughout the maddening imagery, its purpose impossible to discern. After flicking through, Jessie took a second look at the folder itself. Written on a small white label, stuck to the front: *Esternati Division of Astral Inquiry - Case File #741.*

"W-what the hell is this p-place?" Elijah approached the mechanical solar system in the middle of the room. Picking it up, he was surprised by how light it was. The device looked vaguely scientific – brass-limbed, gear-toothed – a clockwork machine with delicate rods, each sprouting from a central pedestal. Planet-like shapes hovered at the end of each branch, though none resembling Earth, Mars, or any other planetary body one might expect. Some were made from smoky glass, others shone like pearls or polished bone. One held a faint glow that grew brighter the longer he stared. At the mechanism's heart, a tiny structure had been carved out of red stone. A building. Towered and terraced, it reminded Elijah of an upside-down mountain, a bee-hive, or perhaps an eastern monastery… It all seemed unsettlingly familiar. A location he couldn't name. A memory from his dreams. A chapter from a book he'd never read yet somehow knew the contents of.

Whatever the hell it was, the red building was a focal point. Something about it dragged you in. Elijah blinked, shaking his head, clearing his mind. For a moment, he considered settling with the device, cross-legged on the floor, swaddling it in his arms like an infant. It yearned for him to whisper to it – a true friend that would hold his secrets safe.

At its base, a bronze plaque stated:

ASTRAL PLANE – CLOSEST SUSPECTED CONFIG-URATION.

The wording itched at him. *Suspected? What the hell did that mean?* The longer he stared, the more the machine seemed to… stare back. The pull came from the device itself, as though it had turned its face toward Elijah, showing him that which he was not meant to see.

"Uh… sis? Y-you should take a look at this…"

The filing cabinet drawer rattled shut as Jessie moved to join him. He could hear her approaching, and yet, he couldn't turn his eyes away. A small, protruding button suddenly made itself known, just above the plaque. Non-existent one moment, always there the next. His finger was on it, pressing. *Is that me?* Elijah questioned. *Is that my hand?*

Then the plaque was gone. A dial flickered to life in its place, tiny numbers shooting past, gradually slowing to stop in a specific order, a casino slot machine.

"Are those coordinates?" Jessie's voice, cutting through. A strange light began to build as the "planets" rotated, the rods turned. Warm. Purple, tainted by narrow veins of sickly green. The relic buzzed, louder and louder, building towards a crescendo. Until…

VWOOOOOOOM!

Energy flooded the room, pulsing forcefully through both twins. They fell to the ground as the light dispersed.

"Ugh… You oka—"

"What the FUCK?"

Jessie turned. Elijah was still next to her, looking at the palms of his hands, his mouth agape. She followed his gaze and froze. His hands were transparent. Ghostly. See-through and phantom-like. It wasn't *just* his hands either. His whole body had transformed like an X-ray with light passing through. Jessie raised her own hands to her face. Glassy. A wave of nausea came over her. Something was seriously wron—

"WHAT THE FUCK?" Elijah screamed again – louder this time. He was losing his grip, panic rising like bile in his throat. His feet were no longer touching the ground. He was in the air, hovering, looking down on himself. Or rather, on his unconscious body which lay motionless on the floor. Jessie recognized herself next to him. Silky, silver cords extended from each of their bellies, trailing upwards, connecting with their levitating forms.

"I-I don't understand."

"Am I dead?" Elijah raised his voice even louder: "Are we fucking dead?"

Jessie placed a spectral hand against his cheek.

"Hey! I'm here! You're okay. We're all good!" A lie. A stammering. The last of her words barely clearing her teeth.

More buzzing. The strange device hovered half a meter above the table. Purple lights turning on, one-by-one, around the device's outer perimeter. Moving through stages. Generating power. Charging up. Charging. Charging. Charging…

"Oh god! It's d-doing it again!"

Elijah attempted a dash for his body, but there was nothing to weigh him down. His sudden movement, instead of taking him to his destination, sent him spiralling, weightless, to the wrong side of the room.

The device erupted again, brighter and more powerful than the first time. An overwhelming spectrum of colors surrounded them. Without warning, a magnetic force pulled, dragging the twins towards the thing. As they neared, it ruptured, opening up into a portal of swirling mist, abducting the DeLuca's into a kaleidoscope of dizzying eldritch motion...

THREE

Cannery Town, Ghostward. Meanwhile…

"**G**etting loud out there," exclaimed the young woman. She lay against a black reclining chair, her left leg exposed and naked all the way to her underwear. The high-pitched buzzing of the tattoo machine filled the space like a speeding wasp. Leaning in, Hunter Garcia pressed down, grinding many needle points in a cross-stich pattern across her skin.

"Yeah," he muttered. "GPD fuckers always draw a crowd."

Stopping, Hunter placed the machine on his work trolley. With a damp paper towel, he wiped away the excess ink. Outside, what little sun afforded to the city that day bled out into grey dusk. The protest in the square showed no sign of dispersing. If anything, the crowd had grown larger in the past hour – a storm surge of angry people and hand-painted signs.

They'd been there most of the day, soaked to the bone, their voices raw and demanding. The people of Ghostward sought answers. This was a familiar ritual in Cannery Town. Once a titan of industry, the neighbourhood sat wedged between the factory and fishmonger districts along the bank of the Ghostward river. In its day, Cannery Town had housed workers for the city's lucrative tinned-food market. Times had changed, and the politicians of City Hall now considered Cannery Town a dumping ground for the poor.

Cheap rent. Even cheaper graves.

Merchants Of Skin, Hunter's studio (well, his boss's, really), squatted on the edge of Central Square, alongside other low-level businesses and Mom 'n Pop stores. It was a good spot – lots of foot traffic – but also a prime location for an angry populace to vent their fury.

"What's the problem this time?" the woman asked, clenching her teeth as Hunter returned to work.

"You haven't heard?"

"I've been out of town a few years. Parents still live here though. I try to visit when I can."

Hunter scoffed. "Hell of a time to come back. Hard to say what kicked this round of crazy off. Weird shit's been stacking up for months. Maybe longer."

"It's Ghostward. Isn't weird just another day?"

"Nah." Hunter shook his head slowly. "Something's changed. Things are worse. The air is heavy. Everyone glancing over shoulders. Nobody's sleeping much – fucked if I know why. Whole city's balanced on a knife's edge."

He wiped again, then dipped the needle. "People are scared. Confused. All sorts of stories floating about. Power surges. Fucked up singing in abandoned buildings. Voices echoing out of kitchen sinks. The Concrete Jungle's even more dangerous than normal, and don't even get me started on all the sightings of… really… big… bugs…"

The woman chuckled nervously. "Bugs, you say?" She glanced back towards the shop window. "You believe any of it?"

Hunter froze. Something shifted, like a drop in pressure. He opened his mouth to speak, but nothing came out. A smell, or the memory of one, passed over his senses, coating the back of his tongue like blood clots and bitter grounds. A foggy mirage from the other night loomed…

Him: Stoned and starving at two AM, meandering towards the falafel place, a pilgrimage and tithe to the god of late-night munchies.

Him again: A side street swathed in shadow; the hair at his nape prickling.

Him: Watched.

Him: Examined.

Him: Dissected.

Up ahead: A big, hulking fucker beneath an abandoned bus stop, slouching. Hooded eyes. Insidious grin.

Too tall to be a regular man.

Teeth too wide and too thick. Off-white bricks, mortared in meat, framed by wide, grinning lips.

Hunter: Shuddering with dread. The voyeur looking on, a slimy black tongue darting in and out of his mouth, making repulsive, sucking and popping clicks against the roof of its gaping maw.

"Hey there, Hunter," the stranger boomed, low and rippling, "why don't you come back here? With me?"

Hunter: Dropping gaze to pavement. *Come on, one step after the other. Keep walking. Keep fucking walking...*

"Awh, don't be afraid! It'll be fun! Let me lick those tight muscles. Let me peel off your skin. Let me clean your bones!"

Hunter: Picking up the pace, staying in the wash of streetlights and their nascent glow...

✿✿✿

By morning, those details were already smudged and smeared. Now, as Hunter tried to recall exactly what had happened, they slipped from his grasp like oil on water.

"You okay, man?" his client asked.

Hunter exhaled. He'd been holding his breath. He blinked, then managed a smile.

"I'm good," he replied. Too quickly. Then, softer: "Doesn't matter if I believe any of it or not. Things have clearly escalated."

He devoted his attention to a small piece of detail, distracting himself with the thin black lines.

"A few local kids have gone missing in the past month or two. GPD says they're run-aways, not worth the resources it'd take to find 'em. And well…" He motioned to the protesters outside. "…clearly not the response everyone was hoping for."

Shaking himself from his strange malaise, Hunter sighed gently. Setting his tools down, he took a moment to admire his work. An intricate pattern of ivy vines arched across the woman's leg.

"Alrighty," he said, "I reckon that's enough for today."

Spraying the wound with a small bottle of saline, Hunter began a final clean of the area, wiping away the pinkish fluid weeping from the piece. He applied an antiseptic ointment before covering her leg with cling wrap.

"Looking good," the woman responded, hoisting herself up in the chair for a better angle.

"Yeah, not too shabby." Hunter smiled. Reaching over to his trolley, he retrieved a small diary and leafed through its pages. "Let's see… We've still got a little bit of shading to do, then a dash of color if you'd like. I've got you down for a final appointment on Tuesday?"

"That's the one."

"Great," he replied, making a note and putting his diary away. "You know the deal. Keep it clean. Out of direct sunlight." He paused, considering the standard weather of Ghostward. "That shouldn't be too much of a problem while you're here."

Laughing, the woman stood, shaking a little with adrenaline.

"You're the man, Hunter," she said, limping towards the front door. "See ya in a few."

Alone now, Hunter started wiping the chair down, getting things ready for closing.

DING!

The entrance bell rang as someone shuffled inside.

"Hey sorry, we're just about to close!" he called without looking up.

"Ah damn. Was hoping for a little smiley face right here… on the left cheek!"

The voice was deep, but youthful, accompanied by the crack of a hand slapping playfully against ass. Hunter rolled his eyes. It was Carlos.

"Hey, *hermano*. What're you doing here?" he asked, locking eyes with the sixteen-year-old standing at his reception.

"*Hola,* big brother," Carlos greeted him, a glint in his eyes, mischief in his smile. He approached the counter, leaned over it and started scanning for loose change.

Ah. So that's why you're here.

The younger Garcia stood slightly shorter than Hunter at 5'9". His shoulder-length, choppy hair was swept to the side in a heavy, textured fringe. They were only half-related – same dead mom, different loser dads – yet to the untrained, they could've been full siblings. Both had their mother's coffee-tinted skin and emerald eyes. Whereas Hunter was slightly bulkier, Carlos was lanky, sinewy, and thin. Ironically, the shit-eating grins both brothers were known for had developed naturally. No genetics required.

Placing the last of his tools away, Hunter joined the kid at the till.

"How's school?"

The boy groaned dramatically. Pulling himself jauntily away from the counter, he spun on his feet, collapsing on a nearby sofa in the reception, and threw his Converse shoes up over the arm rest.

"Really, bro? How's school? You one of the adults now?"

"Okay. Fuck school then. How's the poetry?"

"Ughhhhh." Carlos groaned for a second time. "Don't even, man. It's been driving me friggen crazy..."

"Oh yeah?"

"For real. I'm having a hell of a time trying to get this last stanza to hit."

"Uh-huh."

"Whole piece is pretty tight. It's almost there. But the rhyme scheme feels fuckin' lame. Like I'm just following a formula, like I ain't being human."

"Well, what's your intention?" Hunter asked.

"I just told you, bro!" Carlos exclaimed, sitting up, drawing his knees – exposed and knobbly through torn jeans – into his chest. "I want it to spiral! Like, build, break, rebuild… A heartbeat skipping. But every time I try to spill it, words either sound forced, or worse… like I'm tryna be fuckin' clever. And I'm not. I'm trying to be *real*."

Hunter nodded.

"If the rhyming's in your way, then ditch it. If it's not saying what you need, then it won't matter whether it's pretty or not. You wanna land a gut punch, right? Don't be afraid to swing big and make a mistake."

"Hey, I ain't afraid! Just… What good's a spoken-word poet if the words are all fucky? They gotta flow."

"Do they?" Hunter asked somewhat antagonistically. "My best lyrics rarely make grammatical sense. They just bleed right. Make them bleed and you're all good, man. People'll dig it."

"Hm."

Both fell into silence. It was awkward, the space between them filling with a question. Hunter cleared his throat, shuffled tattoo magazines on the counter, and asked,

"So why are you really here?"

"Oh, uh… I was hoping you might be able to help me out with a bit of cash?" the teenager asked. "Big bro looking out for little bro, y'know?"

"Has Mami Lena stopped giving you an allowance?" Carlos scrunched up his face.

"She's dropping what she can, but… dude! She's poor. And ancient! Plus, that Catholic guilt runs strong, man. The old bat won't even let me buy sour gummy worms. Thinks they're possessed by the demon of tooth decay or something!"

"Duh! Gummy worms. Gum. Worms. Rot your teeth … and then your SOUL!"

"Oh, ha, ha. Very funny. You don't have to live with it though. Last week I asked her for a few bucks to take this chick out on a date. Woman gave me a prayer card and a lecture on abstinence instead."

"I mean, you *are* kinda horny all the ti—"

"Not the point!"

"She's probably just trying to stop you from turning into me."

"Jeez, that *would* be a nightmare!" Carlos laughed.

"Maaaybe go easy on her, aye?" Hunter replied. "Mami Lena's not as uptight as you think."

"I find that hard to believe."

Stepping out from behind the counter, Hunter retrieved his denim jacket from the coat hanger near the doors. Sliding it over his shoulders, he continued.

"She was fighting in the jungle at your age."

"Liar."

"I'm serious. Back when she still had *both* her knees, Mami Lena was a *guerillera* during *La Violencia*. Kicked fascist butt all through her early twenties."

"No shit?"

"She was seventeen when the Conservatives started killing our family. So, she picked up a rifle and joined the resistance."

"Still won't let me buy Hot Cheetos though."

"Gotta learn to embrace the mystery, dude." Hunter chuckled, flipping the studio's sign to *closed*.

"Anyway, let's bounce. You still skate? I've got a spare board out back if you want."

Carlos' eyes lit up.

"¿Y el agua no moja o qué?"

The two stepped out onto the wet pavement and immediately into the crowd of protestors. Down the block, the parade had expanded from Central Square and into the surrounding streets. Raw-throated chants echoed off the concrete buildings and reinforced glass. Hunter pulled a battered old deck from his backpack. Despite the worn and ragged grip tape, this deck was special to him. He'd bought it when he first moved back from New Zealand seven years ago. Skating had been the thing that he and Carlos bonded over, after not seeing each other since Carlos was a toddler. Many things were different since that day, but their shared passion for grazed elbows and half pipes had only grown stronger. Carlos spun one of the wheels on Hunter's spare board with a lone finger, holding it close to observe the smoothness of its movement. This deck was a fresher one, adorned with the image of Bart Simpson on the underside. The trucks clacked lightly as he dropped it to the pavement.

Zipping up his jacket, Hunter kicked off, weaving through the crowd at a cautious roll. Carlos pushed off beside him.

"There's an ATM just past Jimmy's Bodega," said Hunter, pointing out a side street leading away from the square. A block of shuttered shops lay on the other side. "How much you need?"

"Uhh, ten bucks alright? I'm meeting Ethan after his basketball practice. Headed to a house gig out in Elmrose. High School bands. Wanna sneak some drinks."

"Hence Mami Lena's closed wallet."

"Right."

The square was choked now, making their skating a bit of a risky game. But the brothers took it as a challenge. They carved through the crowd, past candles flickering at the base of a rain-slicked statue. Some Confederate bastard nobody remembered, standing tall in its bronze racism. They slowed as the terrain got tighter, navigating between legs and plastic chairs, each board reverberating quietly on the wet asphalt.

Close by, a loudspeaker crackled, giving way to the gritty words of a moody cop. A cop who was *definitely not* reading from a script.

"Alright, listen up, everybody," the officer began, but as soon as he spoke, a furious voice within the crowd interjected.

"WHY SHOULD WE? WHO THE HELL ARE YOU?"

Taken aback, the officer ran his hand nervously through his silver hair.

"My name is Detective Malone," he started, "I'm the chief investigator on this ca—"

"WHERE ARE OUR KIDS?" another voice shouted from the back, irate.

Malone grimaced and tried again.

"I'm the chief investi—"

"YOU THINK CALLING THEM RUNAWAYS MAKES IT OKAY NOT TO DO YOUR JOB?"

Murmurs began to surge in the crowd. Then another frustrated cry. "AND WHO KEEPS CHANGING THE STREET SIGNS AT NIGHT?"

Malone paused, taken aback.

"Are you sure you're not just getting confu—"

"I'VE LIVED HERE TWENTY-FIVE YEARS! I KNOW WHERE ROSEWOOD MEETS VERNON, YOU ARROGANT BASTARD!"

"Sir, I'd ask you not to cuss at m—"

"I heard bricks moving last night in my apartment hallway!" a woman declared to those around her with a raised voice. "Like the walls were breathing! Now I can't find my cats anywhere!"

"Screw your cats, lady!" another voice roared. "My daughter's been missing for over a week!"

Hunter watched from the corner of his eye as the crowd began to move again, tightening around the cop at his podium. They were mothers, teachers, dedicated members of the neighborhood watch. There were even a few faces Hunter recognized from the Scene. Real people. Real rage. Their murmuring grew jagged. Voices rising in confusion and fear. Flammable. A single spark and the rocks would start flying. Detective Malone looked out across the crowd, backing away from them, his lips twitching.

Something was happening in Ghostward.

Something nobody seemed prepared to admit.

Maybe it'd always been happening.

Maybe it was already too late.

Carlos kicked his board up into his hand as they reached the edge of the square. They ducked past a line of fold-out tables and into the side street leading to the next block. He glanced over his shoulder, eyes resting temporarily on Detective Malone, then back to Hunter.

"I'm surprised you're not up front with a fuckin' megaphone," he said. "FIRE AND FURY," the teen announced, throwing his spare arm out in front of them like he was announcing a setlist. "THE OUTRAGE! *Live, unplugged and pissed-the-fuck-off!*"

Hunter stared into the distance. It was coming down hard now, raindrops turning puddles into pools of angry ripples. The harsh weather made it easier for him – thousands of pitter-patters filling the silence. He kicked gently, coasting alongside his half-brother as they passed through the alley. A current of water rushed through the gutter to his left, carrying little boats of trash into the sewers below.

"Don't really see much point *hermano*," Hunter said eventually. "Yelling at a system that doesn't give two shits gets you nothing more than a migraine and sore throat."

Carlos frowned but didn't press. Hunter could sense him watching, though. The high schooler's eyes were heavy on him – not judgemental, more… inquisitive. Concerned. That was the thing about brothers – even half ones. You could lie to them all you liked, but they were masters at hearing the truth behind your words.

Hunter clenched his jaw, running a free hand through his soggy hair. He'd screamed himself hoarse too many nights to count. Thrashing and wailing about revolution his entire adult life, only to walk home through the same broken streets, enduring the same broken life he'd always lived. Ghostward never changed. Not for him. Not for anyone. In fact, Hunter had taken to wondering lately if, for all his screaming, for all the blast-beats, two-steps, and breakdowns, he was just feeding something else – an anger that was infinitely hungry, that could never truly be satisfied.

"You reckon dude's spinning shit then?" asked Carlos, jabbing a thumb back towards the square, where Detective Malone was undoubtedly trying to vacate the podium before the crowd totally surrounded him.

"I think he's telling the version of the truth that he hopes will cause the least amount of trouble," Hunter replied. "Seems like it's going well."

Seconds later, the two found themselves on the next footpath, free from the crowd. Carlos smirked.

"Race you to the bodega?"

The kid didn't wait for confirmation. He kicked hard, once, twice – his baggy hoodie flaring behind like a parachute – and took off down the block.

Hunter hesitated just long enough to be annoyed, then bent low and pushed after him, his wheels skimming puddles and kicking up sideway trails of muddy water. Up ahead, Carlos weaved between busted sidewalk panels and graffiti-tagged trash cans like he owned the street.

"Cheater!" Hunter called out to him, but Carlos only laughed. He threw a sloppy peace sign over his shoulder before dropping a finger and flipping Hunter off.

In front of them, a low guardrail lined the curb. Carlos hit it clean, grinding fast and loud, metal shrieking against metal, before dropping down with a wobbly landing. He whooped triumphantly, shooting a cocky glance back at Hunter.

"Beat that!"

Hunter snorted through his teeth, bombing the same line, only faster. He hit the grind smoother, leaning into it with his weight. He landed tight, bent low, and used the speed he'd gained to circle around his half-brother, shoulder-checking him as he passed.

Stumbling, nearly falling from his deck, Carlos caught himself at the last moment, recovering and hooning forward in pursuit.

"Hey! Don't be an ass!"

Chuckling, Hunter flicked his board into a front shove and rolled backward for a second, coasting, breathing harder now. His chest ached, not from exertion, but from the ghost of something older, lodged beneath his sinew.

They reached the mouth of the block, boards slowing as they turned the corner. The glow of an ATM next to Jimmy's Bodega came into view. The sandwich shop was a mainstay in this part of the city, usually busy from dawn till dusk. This evening, however, its windows were already shuttered. Jimmy had gone for the night. Back to his wife and four kids. A liquor store sat on the other side of the cash machine, covered in tattered flyers, job adverts, and fuzzy photos of shoplifters caught on camera. Carlos let his board come to a stop. Stepping off, defeated, he joined his brother in front of the digital screen.

Inserting his card and plugging in a pin number, Hunter navigated through the chunky green-on-black interface, clacking buttons like an old remote. The machine clattered. A moment later, two ten dollar bills spat out into his waiting hand. Hunter folded them together and shoved both into Carlos' fist.

"Twenty? Thanks, bro. You're the man!"

Hunter smiled and ruffled the younger Garcia's hair.

"Hope not. Aren't we supposed to stick it to that guy?"

"Yeah, but let's save that for another time. I gotta head out."

INTERLUDE

Sterling Courts, Northeast Ghostward. Meanwhile…

The chain-link fence rattled in the early evening wind. On the other side, a scrappy group of teenage boys sprinted across a basketball court, their voices bouncing and echoing against the decaying façade of Sterling Tower Residences. Sneakers squeaked as the orange ball thudded against the Tarmac.

Ethan was the smallest kid here. Fifteen, scrawny, with narrow shoulders and pale, freckled arms, the march through puberty had been more of a slow walk for him. His hair – naturally red – was bleached down to the roots and buzzed short, a home-job haircut over a kitchen sink. His slightly protruding ears were stretched and adorned with two slim, silver tunnels. He wore an oversized Snapcase hoodie, which clung, sopping wet, to his frame. Watching him move, it was clear Ethan hustled twice as hard to keep up with the other boys on the team.

Darting across the court, Ethan watched the ball skid along the backboard with a hollow smack, rebounding wide and scooped up almost instantly by a kid from the opposing team. The boy, tall and muscular, pivoted on his feet, scanning, then launched a pass downcourt. The ball sailed through the drizzle-heavy air before slapping into the hands of another near the three-point line.

Sensing an opportunity, Ethan bolted after him.

Having trailed behind all quarter, playing catch-up with the older kids, Ethan now pushed forward. His lungs flared as his feet slid through puddles. The guy with the ball saw him coming and refused to slow. Ethan approached, a tiny voice screaming in his head for him to turn the other direction and run. The dude coming at him was built like a full-grown man! Already shaving, already broad across the shoulders. The way he moved was a declaration, the challenge of a player who'd clearly done this hundreds of times before. Two steps, then a launch and he was airborne.

Ethan powered forward to meet him.

But he was too slow, too light. His arms flailed upwards, reaching for the ball as it blew past him, slamming through the hoop with a metallic crack. The chain net snapped like the jaw of a sewer alligator. One of the opposing kids let out a victory whoop.

"Yeah! Go big, Leon!"

Ethan landed hard and off balance. His sneakers squealed. He refused to look at the others. Instead, he doubled over, hands on his thighs, breathing through the stitch radiating across his ribcage. His calf-muscles burned with exertion, and his cheeks flushed bright pink. Ethan wasn't the worst player. But he was the lightest. Every collision sent him flying. The older boys didn't slow down for him, and nobody clapped when he got back up. Not that he expected them to. That was the whole point of training with kids a year older. A trial by fire. He'd eventually get better, grow stronger, but it'd be a hard slog. The ball rolled across the court, coming to rest in front of him. Picking it up, Ethan passed immediately to another player and stepped to the sideline.

Shortly after, as the players called the game and started to peel off home, Leon came up behind Ethan and smacked a hand across his back in a friendly gesture.

"Don't sweat it, little man. You played a good game."

Ethan nodded and smiled slightly in response.

"Thanks."

Some of the other players filed past them, out the gate. They were teasing each other, still high of the rush of the game. One shouted something about stopping for burgers, another suggested heading over to the arcade on Weave Street, but ultimately, the group decided – like most teens – on food.

Leon jerked his thumb after them. "Sounds like some of us are gonna grab a bite. You in?"

Ethan shook his head, turning back to the court. "Nah, I'm good," he replied. "Meeting a friend."

"Alright, my man." Leon grinned, slapping Ethan's back again. "Maybe get in some practice while you wait, huh?" He tossed Ethan the ball, and then, turning to the others out on the footpath, "Yo, dudes, wait up!"

With the others gone, Ethan walked back across the court, dribbling the ball alone in the fading light. Lining up a shot, he bounced on his heels and flung the orange globe, watching with unsurprised disappointment as it swung around the rim of the hoop before tumbling pointlessly to the ground. Ethan hissed through his teeth, rushing the ball and kicking it hard.

"Bullshit!"

The ball bounced before rolling towards the edge of the court. It was stopped by a foot. No. Not a foot. A soft ripple in the dark. A figure stood there above the ball.

Ethan squinted. At first, the stranger looked more like a silhouette peeled from a crumbling wall – a human shape smudged in soot. The dark-man. Light seemed to curve around him. A thin draft slid across the court towards Ethan. The boy was still panting slightly and so the draft passed quickly into his lungs. It coated his tongue with the taste of batteries, filled the nasal cavities with smoke and bitter persistence.

Still, something about this was calming…Warm, even. The semi-lucid state just before sleep, wrapped in a thick blanket. Ethan's pulse slowed even as his mind tried to make sense of what stood before him.

Bending over, the dark-man retrieved Ethan's ball for him and cradled it under one arm. Coiling smoke rose from him like dancing finger bones.

"Keep at it, kid," the dark-man said. His voice oozed like molasses, slow and warm. Enveloping. All-encompassing.

"Persistence is key."

Ethan blinked.

Everything inside his skull screamed for him to run. He knew better than to stay. He knew better than to talk to strangers in Ghostward. And now that he was facing this… person? This… thing?

His legs refused to move. The boy was glued to the spot. He wanted to scream. To yell. To call for help. Instead, when his mouth finally did open, he heard his own words like they belonged to another:

"Uh, thanks, I guess?"

No. That's not right. That wasn't what I meant to say.

The dark-man's chest shook slightly, a polite laugh.

"No problem."

Tell him to back off. Tell him you want nothing to do with this creep. Get the fuck away and never come back here! Say it!

"Can I have my ball back now?"

What the fuck?

The dark-man startled, waking from a thought.

"Oh! Yes. Of course."

He held out the basketball in both hands, waiting for Ethan to approach.

Don't do it dude. Don't take the ball.

Ethan stepped slowly forward. He reached out. The dark-man's face remained hidden beneath his low-drawn hood of moving black. He was watching Ethan. Staring. Studying. Admiring.

"You hungry?" the figure asked as soon as Ethan made contact with the ball. "Got pizza in my car just over there." He motioned nowhere in particular. "Can never finish one on my own." He laughed.

Ethan paused. "Car? What car?"

To this, the dark-man let loose a childish giggle. He stifled it, then waited for Ethan's reply.

The question lingered. Pressured. Part of him wanted to say yes. Agreeing felt easier than resisting. *NO! SAY NO! GET AWAY FROM THIS PSYCHO!* At last, Ethan's instincts managed to cut through the trance. He tightened his grip on the ball and tugged.

"Nah, dude. I'm good."

The dark-man didn't let go.

"Oh, come on," he cooed, "It's pepperoni!"

"I'm vegan."

The dark-man yanked back. Suddenly. In a mini-tantrum.

Ethan stumbled, falling hard to his hands and knees, the asphalt skinning his palms.

"What the fuck is your problem?" Ethan barked, scrambling to his feet. "Hng—"

A sharp sting at the side of his neck.

Shock.

This can't be happening. This can't be happening. This can't be happening. This can't be happening.

The dark-man held in one hand a large syringe.

This can't be happening. This CAN'T BE HAPPENING.

Something cold – a liquid – coursing through him, racing to his heart, to his brain.

"…the hell?"

Everything was in slow motion.

A dream? No. This was real. This WAS happening.

Groggy, but brimming with panic, Ethan closed a fist and attempted to swing at his attacker. The dark-man backstepped him with ease. Off balance once more, Ethan collapsed. Things faded, but he tried to form some final words.

"Whaowww da fuck youow do ta me?"

Kneeling to look Ethan in the eyes, the stranger stroked him softly on the cheek, his face shifting and mushrooming like a Rorschach test – the kind Ethan and Carlos had joked over in the school sick bay only recently. *CARLOS! I'm sup… meet… Carlo…*

"Hey, hey. It's okay. Just stay calm," mused the dark-man. "Don't worry, kid. I know your friends. I know those twins. They sent me to get you. Everything's gonna be A-okay…"

Twi….s… wha…?

As Ethan lost consciousness, the dark-man leant in, finally taking a moment to appreciate his catch.

"Tell me, Ethan," he muttered, a perverse tenderness to his voice, "will *you* be my friend?"

FOUR

Jessie was falling.

Or rising upwards.

She couldn't tell which.

Whatever that device was, with its strange whirring noises and unsettling light, it'd done the impossible. Somehow, she'd been split. She couldn't explain it, or how. Almost instinctively, new details about the nature of the world were emerging in her mind, as if she'd always known them. Her real body, the one made of meat and breath – lay curled somewhere, lightyears away, tucked inside her father's hidden room.

But that place wasn't here. Wasn't where she found herself now.

As a multitude of colors, shapes and sounds swirled past her, Jessie looked down to her stomach. The silver umbilical cord still trailed from her belly button, out behind her and into the distance. As it got further away, the cord became a blur, a streak, like a test-swab of metallic paint, stretched way too thin. She couldn't see where it went once it faded out, but a faint heartbeat pulsed through the connection like a vibrating guitar string.

Elijah was nowhere to be seen. They'd locked eyes briefly before the device did its thing, but now, he was gone. Jessie was on her own, sailing at hyper-speed through a place that was not a place. A tunnel that was not a tunnel. An ocean that was not the sea. Reaching out with her thoughts, she grasped at distant whispers. Her brother. He was unseen, but Jessie sensed his presence. He was both beside her, and impossibly far away. Like staring into a mirror too long, Elijah was the reflection looking back, independent of her and equally confused.

Continuing forward at breakneck speed, Jessie tore through the dream space, vast and bottomless. Great eruptions of stardust twisted around her like cathedral smoke, veined with impossible shades – jade eclipsing mauve, blood-light blooming with folds of pale gold and muddied crimson. The horizon ahead curled in on itself, and Jessie discovered she was not so much moving *through* space as she was somehow pushing *against* it, pulled forward by an unseen presence.

Mountains of memory drifted by. Crumbling towers of half-formed ideas and faceless crowds, each tittering in languages unable to be pronounced by human tongues. Disguised beneath this melting pot of archetypes and obscured revelation, raw currents of dream flowed: hungry, luminous, and infinitely ancient. The shapes around Jessie made her gasp in awe. They weren't made from stone, or gas, or any other configuration of matter taught to her in class. Rather, these were beliefs made solid, a universal spine of forgotten myths, each trailing out and away from one supreme source.

Maybe she was about to encounter this thing. This nexus point, this center of existence. Perhaps that was what was slowly unveiling in the distance – a churning black wound on the horizon that drew all light and energy around it into a cosmic vacuum. In any other situation, such a thing might terrify her, but right now, right here, Jessie found the black hole inviting. It reached out with warmth and… something else. A feeling she couldn't quite place. Seduction, maybe? No. Close. But not the one.

She collided with the black hole and sank, black tar bubbling up around her, embracing and pulling her deeper in, until at last, any sense of independence, of *self-being*, was gone…

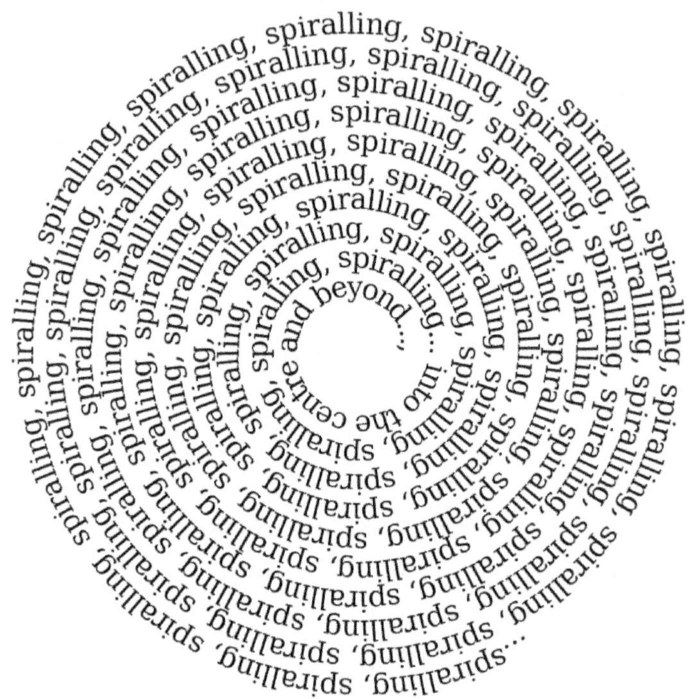

An explosion. An eruption of jagged, bolted electricity passing through her. Each stab violent, painful. The sensation continued for what could have been an eternity, before suddenly, it ceased. Now, it was like Jessie was passing through water. No. Not water. Something thick and dense, both dry and wet, bitter and sweet. Jessie breached the surface, tumbling through smoke and static, symbols etched in flame and opened wrists. Time became a knot. Meaning peeling away like old paint. And then...

walls bleeding from mortar stages stages shadows
turning no eyes rigid slithering slithering dry curling shapes
shapes blinking back hissing hissing symbols in black mist
on crumbling brick man shapes void hungry obsessed
arms outstretching

figure figure labial mouth creeping erupt
ega guincaer slow descending teeth impossible guincaer
like nourishment flying moth exploding star above the
vast faceless lung pit pit bodies convulsing rhythm limbs
limbs flailing fists fists

collapsing bells bells ringing sonce growing louder
louder shriek tower tower tolling brick bong shiver rocks
tumbling fog

never stopping never stopping tubes tubes wrapping like
thorns creeping creeping never stopping broken glass
scree scree no mouth resounding marrow boy not yet
man no bog fist bruised bloody pounding parental glass
womb womb floating sterile void void container

blood glitter glitter radiator formation formation smoke
shapes bursting ghosts ghosts soaring organized violence
plastic rapture plastic shields advancing formation
gushing teeth iron bong conformity in blue cloth fire
across city skyline shadows torn hoories hurling brick riot
consuming immense immense blistering rage blooming
blooming

*summoning decoming Honbs Helb qalm dearing odjects
not odjects not odjects moonlight Hoobed ƚibures still as
sdrawpu buinnur xaw selbuac elcric seutats statuse circle circle canbles wax running uqwarbs
uqwarbs*

*bngles crreaming crreaming lanbroabqes dlinking
dlinking crookƨb qeaometry itching draing draing boorwoys
oqening oosmic qillars stitcheb with runes olb as draeth
draeth emqty ruins ruins snow on mountains mountains
towering doots on gravel bereat saubs bereat saubs with
slows slows toqqing sqaeoking Hen noms grinning grinning
walking on Hinb lags like a ekil man jackal dloakening taugs
taugs oleon inviting inviting*

She fell again, deeper. Blood. A fluorescent flicker that radiated down from rotten heavens. There before her – him. Hunter. Doubled over in pain, pinned against a cracked concrete pillar, his white singlet shredded and soaked in gore. Hunter's arms mostly limp, but his fists tightened in defiance around a thick black appendage, pocked with scars and tiny tendrils. He looked up, one eye swollen shut, his thin lips rimmed with red. Around the scene, countless whispering continued to murmur in reverse.

"Any last words?" the voice of another, coming from nowhere. Old. Amused. Muffled. Maybe male, maybe female, maybe human, perhaps something worse.

Hunter's one good eye slowly focused in on the speaker. A grim smile, drowned in ichor.

"Yeah," he replied, spitting gooey pink saliva to the ground. "…*Me cago en la crica de la puta que te parió.*"

The vision ended abruptly. Hunter's face blinked out of existence.

Jessie lurched forward, gasping, filling her lungs with polluted air. Without any warning, she was back. Hovering several inches above the wood-panelled floor, her body laid out in front of her, sleeping. It was curious that even separate from her physical form, Jessie felt the need to breathe. Did a metaphysical projection even have lungs? Perhaps even apart from one's self, old habits died hard. Her final vision surged back – looping, glitching – re-runs of the worst TV show she could imagine.

"Hunter!"

The vision flittered through her synapses. Her heart ached. Jessie had wounded him when their romance ended. It'd been a hard time in both their lives. She'd lashed out at those nearest, extracting what had been her attempt at vengeance. Faced with this prophecy, Jessie wanted desperately to hug him. She'd been a total bitch the other week at the show, and like a champ, Hunter took it on the chin. He'd reached out and she'd shut him down. He kept his smile, of course. Hunter always did that when it came to her. But she'd seen it. The tiny grey glimmer of crushed hope. She needed to visit him, see him, if she ever got out of this mess. Rocking up at Merchants of Skin, she'd rush through the shop doors, past the counter, into the back room and find him there, dutifully sanitizing equipment. She'd catch him by surprise and sink into his muscular arms. He'd be alarmed at first. Fight or flight. Then, he'd click. Those arms would tighten around her. Their eyes would connect. She'd lean forward, pressing her lips against his, running her palm across his scratchy stubble, as her tongue danced with his.

The fantasy vanished abruptly. Jessie checked on her brother. He was still asleep. Floating above them both, she looked over to the table in the middle of the room. The device – that otherworldly thing responsible for whatever-the-fuck-this-was – was gone. Its absence set off a cascade of questions. What was it? How had it done what it did? Where had it gone? Had it been taken? By whom? Were they alone? Was someone else here?

She scanned the room, but there was nobody. Just them, the dust and the gloom. Not that this eased Jessie's fears in the slightest. Something was out there. Another presence. Not Elijah's. Not her own. Hostile. Nearby. Not in the room. Not in the apartment either. Outside. Steadily approaching like the intimidating echo of a bass-heavy car stereo blocks away.

"I'll be right back," she promised Elijah.

Jessie willed herself forward, feeling her movement like learning to swim. Flying out of the secret room, she headed for the windows of her father's study. Upon reaching the tattered blinds, she kept moving, the wooden slats passing through her, followed by glass, then open air. She was outside now, high above the city, taking in the blinking neon haze. The wind whistled around her, failing to freeze her skin. She was still a part of this world, and yet, somehow... isolated from it. Several stories below, Jessie's little run-down car sat vacant like a dark blotch on paper. A puff of cloud wafted by, reminding her of how high up she was. But any fear that might accompany this kind of realization was missing. Exhilaration had replaced it.

A few seconds passed as she took in the view. Then, remembering why it was she was out here, she centred her focus. The hostile presence. Closer now, a black van tearing into the parking lot below. Swerving violently as it pulled in, the van sped towards Waldorf Tower. It came to a screeching halt just outside. The officer on guard darted from beneath the awning, weapon drawn. He shouted something to the driver, but his words were lost in the rain. As the cop reached the van, the carpark lit up. A single flash of green light pulsed out from the vehicle, flinging the officer backwards. Dead before he even hit the ground. Several men piled out, dressed in expensive corporate-style attire. They powered past the officer's corpse, entering the tower.

Fuck.

There was no time. Whoever those assholes were, Jessie could guess their destination. She and Elijah needed to be gone by the time they reached the apartment. She had to get back. Had to wake her brother up. Had to somehow get them both into their bodies and gone.

She only had minutes, at most…

FIVE

A light flickered in the dark. Sporadic flashes, faint radio signals wavering then settling. Elijah opened his eyes. He was on his side, his cheek pressed uncomfortably into dirt. Small pieces of rubble dug into his skin, sticking to it, creating indentations. A soft electrical hum filled the air. Groaning, he rolled, moving onto his back to face the churning sky. It was different. More vibrant and real than any he'd ever seen at home. A painted world like those his father had shown him years ago, in the Louvre.

Elijah pulled himself into a sitting position. Fragmented remains of ancient pillars stood around him. At first glance, they reminded him of Greek or Roman architecture, but looking closer, their surfaces twisted subtly.

"J-Jessie?"

But his sister was gone. Their father's study was gone. Waldorf Tower, gone. Ghostward? MIA. Shaking off his disorientation, Elijah forced himself up. The air crackled. He stood atop a rugged slope. A large hill, or maybe even a small mountain. Thick, ruddy grass grew around his feet. Stepping away from the ruins towards the edge, Elijah looked out at the horizon. Below him, rolling meadows, overgrown with rows upon rows of lavender, sprawled in an endless expanse. Their fragrant blooming filled the air with a dense, sleepy perfume. His heart raced. His fingers twitched at his sides. Words stacked in his throat, each one tripping over the next.

Breathtaking, is it not?

The voice was a cold wind: ancient, cracked and heavy. Not so much a sound as an intrusion, worming its way into his mind like an errant dream. Elijah spun, his heart pounding harder.

A figure loomed amidst the ruins. She was monolithic, her presence both majestic and grotesque. Her face – or what Elijah presumed to be her face – shrouded by a mask. A swirling lattice of bone, gold, and stone, carved into countless overlapping visages, each rippling and shifting, trapped in a vortex of emotion. One expression held brief dominion, then melted into the next, rotating: agony, ecstasy, rage, and love… All cycling fluidly across the mask. Where her eyes might have been, two violet pinpricks of light shimmered. They burned with a fierce intensity, piercing him through. Rising up from behind her head, two curved horns spiralled like gnarled branches.

Her upper body was bizarre. What wasn't obscured by robes was translucent and crystalline. Flesh like polished quartz, catching faint rays of sunlight, causing shimmering rainbows to frolic around her. Underneath her skin, opalescent veins throbbed softly. In this, she was beautiful.

Her torso, however, was unnervingly elongated, impossibly elegant and undeniably alien. From her chest rose six exposed breasts, glistening like polished marble. Each nipple stuck out, sharp and pointed. Her multi-jointed arms moved with deliberate grace, talons of black glass extending from each. The lower half of her body, an afterthought, forced like chains upon her. From the waist down, the entity was a quagmire of jagged stone which crept up her legs, locking her in place. Damp moss and lichen clung to the surface.

You've finally come. The entity tilted her head towards Elijah with curiosity, her mask changing again, her face rippling with excitement. She began to move towards him, dragging herself forward with her clawed hands. The stone encasing her lower half groaned against the dirt. Each motion sent shards of petrified flesh across the ground. Ribbons of golden sparks trailing from wrists and shoulders. To Elijah, it was as if this creature was phasing in and out of existence right in front of him. A kind of insanity-induced hallucination.

His legs trembled. The storm above roared louder, though no rain fell. The entity drew closer to him.

I have waited so long, she cooed. *Here, in this place. In the Venusberg…*

She reached out, yearning to touch.

Come. Come closer and let me look upon you, o' blessed incarnation, o' SHEHID-CHETAN. The powerful current rippling from her claws brushed softly against Elijah's face. They weaved between the individual strands of muscle under his skin, playing whimsically with the countless atoms and subatomic particles that made him *him*.

Elijah pulled away, stumbling, his legs quaking. He tripped, hitting the ground hard. Scrambling, he bolted again, his chest tightening. He needed his inhaler. He needed to breathe. He did not look back. Could not look back. The grinding of the entity's body continued slowly in the background. Elijah didn't know what she was, but he was certain that if she caught him, only disaster would follow. Before he could rationalize his actions, he roared and threw himself over the precipice.

The wind howled in his ears as he plummeted towards the fields. Flowers rushed to meet him. But there was no crash. No impact. No pain. He gasped sharply, his body convulsing, his eyes snapping open.

He was back.

In his father's hidden room.

"Eli! Wake up! Please!"

Jessie was shouting at him, gripping his shoulders, shaking him as hard as she could.

"Come on! We have to leave!"

Still disorientated, he tried to sit, but the scene around him came into focus far too quickly. Jessie was crouched, her face pale. The slamming of boots against wooden floors surrounded them. People. Several men moving into view. Sleek, monochromatic outfits. Hair slicked back in stylish cuts. The cold glint of guns as each trained their guns on the twins.

"Where is it?" the leader asked, stepping to the front of his team. He was gaunt like a skeleton. Dark bags clung to his eyes but not from lack of sleep. They were burst blood vessels and swelling sinew, his freshly broken nose contrasting against his outfit's perfection. In fact, all of these men looked like they'd recently lost a fight. A nasty one at that.

Elijah's blood hammered. Give him a million years, and he'd have never guessed when he awoke at the Horizon Behavioural Clinic this morning he'd be staring down the barrel of a gun before the sun had set. But here he was. He wanted to cry and then faint. Jessie's grip on his arm tightened.

The leader jerked his weapon in the twin's faces again.

"Where is it?" he roared. "What have you done with the Astral Orrery?"

To Be Continued...

CORE CAST OF CHARACTERS

(IN ORDER OF APPEARANCE)

One of the sole-survivors of the terrorist attack on Ghostward's Esternati Chapter House, Sam Lockart is both studious and tough. Raised in the Esternati Order, she quickly rose through its ranks and became the prodigy of David DeLuca, its last Compatriota (leader.) Hoping to honor her former mentor's wishes, Sam is determined to survive her plight and aid his children, Jessie and Elijah, in this new, terrifying world they now find themselves in.

Future co-founder of the FBP, Jessie is a young woman with an axe to grind. Twin sister to Elijah, she is the more direct of the two, but also less emotionally available. She cares deeply for her brother and sees herself as his protector – whether he likes it or not! Jessie joined the local hardcore scene in her teens. She was part of the original line-up for THE OUTRAGE, but after a failed romance with its vocalist, Hunter Garcia, she opted to leave and do her own thing.

Future co-founder of the FBP, Elijah is a troubled young man with a nervous disposition and a persistent stutter. Twin brother to Jessie, Elijah is the more emotionally vulnerable of the two. He doesn't know it yet, but Elijah is far more attuned to the supernatural than most. With no one to explain this to him, he has suffered over many years with what he perceived to be severe mental health issues.

Lead singer of THE OUTRAGE and an old friend of Jessie and Elijah's, Hunter is a young Colombian man who immigrated to Ghostward after spending his childhood in New Zealand. A bit of a blunt object, Hunter hits hard and asks questions later. He may look tough and unapproachable but is a big softy at heart and a romantic, to boot. Despite the upsetting ending to his relationship with Jessie, Hunter still harbours feelings for her and is hopeful of a second chance one day.

The younger half-brother of Hunter Garcia, sixteen-year-old Carlos is a bit of a newbie to the hardcore scene. Eager, raw, and burning to prove himself amongst his peers, Carlos can't help but live in the shadow of his brother and the infamy of THE OUTRAGE. But Carlos also has his own voice. A gifted spoken-word poet, he has an almost supernatural knack for silencing others with his powerful lyricism. Charismatic and driven by empathy, Carlos connects deeply with others, even as he battles with feeling like an imposter to the scene.

Ethan Bennick is Carlos' oldest and closest friend. Fifteen years old and already dealing with trauma beyond his years, Ethan became close with both the Garcias and DeLucas shortly after an untimely death in his family. Ethan has a love of basketball, though no matter how much he practices, he can't quite get his skills to the level of his peers. This is a common theme in his life, and Ethan often feels inadequate around those who he looks up to.

BOOK 3:

THROWDOWN AT WALDORF TOWER